W9-CHV-812

WITHDRAWN

VIKING KESTREL

Viking Penguin Inc., 40 West 23rd Street, New York, New York 10010, U.S.A.
Penguin Books Canada Limited, 2801 John Street, Markham, Ontario, Canada L3R 1B4

First published in Great Britain by Andersen Press Limited, 1987
First American Edition
Published in 1988

Printed in Italy

1   2   3   4   5   92   91   90   89   88

Library of Congress catalog card number: 87-40232
(CIP data available)
ISBN 0-670-81971-9

To Sylvie, Sophie, Timothy and Ginger White

Our House on the Hill
Philippe Dupasquier

Viking Kestrel

January

February

March

April

May

July

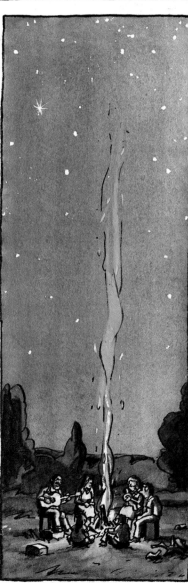

August

September

October

November

December